OLD TOM

This book belongs to.....

. . . .

PUFFIN BOOKS

PUFFIN BOOKS

OLD TOM

Written and Illustrated by

Leigh HOBBS

Puffin Books
Penguin Books Australia Ltd
487 Maroondah Highway, PO Box 257
Ringwood, Victoria 3134, Australia
Penguin Books Ltd
Harmondsworth, Middlesex, England
Viking Penguin, A Division of Penguin Books USA Inc.
375 Hudson Street, New York, New York 10014, USA
Penguin Books Canada Limited
10 Alcorn Avenue, Toronto, Ontario, Canada M4V 3B2
Penguin Books (N.Z.) Ltd
182-190 Wairau Road, Auckland 10, New Zealand

First published by Penguin Books Australia, 1994
10 9 8 7 6 5 4 3 2 1

Typeset in 15/19 pt Bembo
Made and printed in Australia by Australian Print Group, Maryborough, Victoria

National Library of Australia
Cataloguing-in-Publication data:

Hobbs, Leigh.
Old Tom.
ISBN 0 14 036979 1.
1. Cats - Juvenile fiction. I. Title.
A823.3

For Ann James and Jenny Melican

Angela Throgmorton lived alone and liked it that way. One day, while doing some light dusting, she heard a knock at the door.

There, on her front step, was a baby monster.

Angela was curious,
so she carried him in ...

and brought him up.

Angela had never fed a baby before,
and what a strange big baby he was!
She called him 'Old Tom'.

Old Tom grew up very quickly. In fact, it wasn't long before he outgrew his playpen.

And when he did, Angela gave him the spare room. It was all clean and neat.

Angela taught Old Tom how to behave.
'Sit up straight!' she would say.
'Elbows off the table.'

'Not too much on your fork.'
'Chew with your mouth closed.'

There was so much to learn.

But Old Tom loved bath time most of all, when he could splash about and make a mess.

He always liked to look his best ...

especially when he went out to play.

At first, Angela ignored Old Tom's childish pranks.

After all, she had things to do and dishes to wash.

But her heart sank when *someone* forgot his manners.

Old Tom *tried* to be good …

though sometimes he was a bit naughty.

'Aren't you a little too old for such things?' Angela Throgmorton often asked.

As the months went by, Angela tried to keep the house tidy.

It wasn't easy, as Old Tom seemed to be everywhere.

There was no doubt about it,

he was a master of disguise.

Sometimes Angela heard strange noises
coming from the kitchen,

and whenever she had guests, Old Tom would drop in unannounced.

Old Tom was out of control.

'When *will* you grow up?' Angela often muttered under her breath.

Sometimes Old Tom went for a little walk to the letterbox.

But Angela thought it best that he stay inside.
'You mustn't frighten the neighbours,'
she would say.

When babies came to visit ...

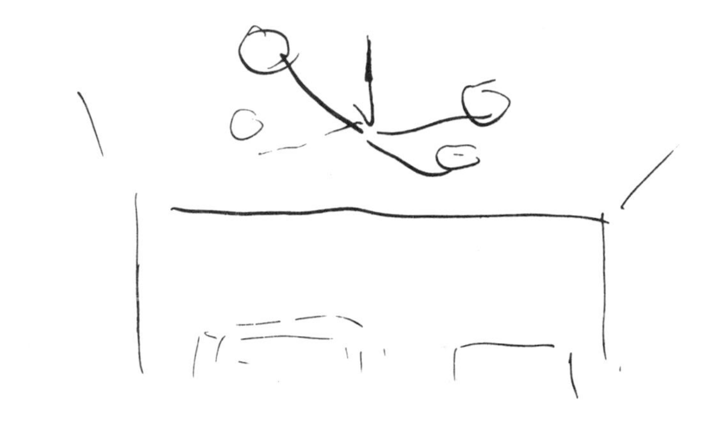

Old Tom loved to play.

‘Heavens, what’s that in the pram
with my baby!’ cried one of Angela’s friends
during afternoon tea one day.

It was Old Tom, of course.
Angela was extremely embarrassed.

By now, Angela was having trouble sleeping.

Her nerves were shattered,

and Old Tom's fur had given her dreadful hayfever.

When she finally did fall asleep, Old Tom was often in her dreams.

Angela longed for the good old days,
when her home was in order ...

with everything in its place.

Whenever it was time to help with the dishes, Old Tom felt sick.

He liked to sleep in, and enjoy a late breakfast on Angela's favourite armchair.

Angela was fed up.

Old Tom had to go.

'At last I have the house to myself!'
cried Angela Throgmorton.

It was a bold move,

but Angela thought it for the best.

Now she was free to scrub ...
and polish,
sweep and mop.

With Old Tom gone, her house would be spick and span once more.

By now Old Tom was in town,

where there were places to see
and people to meet.

In a pet shop nearby, he found new friends to play with.

Some had feathers and one had fins.

But Fluffy the puppy was
Old Tom's favourite.

In the cinema next door the film had just started.

When Old Tom wandered in ...

he was mistaken for a monster on the screen.

CINEMA.
Tickets
THE FURRY BEAST FROM BEYOND

It was a wonderful surprise when
Old Tom found Happyland.

There were swings and slides,

places to hide,

children to play with ...

and an elephant to ride.

Old Tom was having a lovely time.

But not everyone was happy in Happyland.

When darkness fell, Old Tom was alone.

And when the storm came, he tried to be brave,

even when the thunder boomed.

For Old Tom there was
no breakfast or lunch,

or afternoon tea ...

while far away, Angela was alone in her clean tidy home.

Old Tom tried and tried to find
someone to play with.

But he couldn't find one friendly face.

There was no fur on her floor, but Angela still couldn't sleep.

And neither could Old Tom.

He had nowhere to go
and nothing to eat,

until at last he found food at the bottom of a bin,

where he dreamt of his warm safe bed.

Angela was worried sick.

For poor Old Tom ...

the future looked bleak.

Suddenly there was a news flash

'ORANGE FURRY MONSTER CAUGHT.

'That monster is my baby!' cried Angela Throgmorton.

In no time at all, she was off to the pound to rescue Old Tom.

'Be quick!' Angela shrieked.

Inside his cage,
Old Tom had just begun to cry,

when suddenly he heard a big voice boom:
'I'm here for my baby!'

Angela was overjoyed.

And so was Old Tom.

AUTHOR PHOTOGRAPH BY FRANCIS REISS

ABOUT LEIGH HOBBS

Leigh Hobbs was born in Melbourne in 1953. After leaving art school, he created Larry and Lizzy Luna, two caricature sculptures for Sydney's Luna Park. Later he turned Melbourne's Flinders Street Station into a ceramic teapot, now in the National Gallery of Victoria.

Many of Leigh's cartoons have appeared in the *Age* and he has illustrated a number of children's books including *Caro's Croc Cafe* and *Mr Knuckles*.

Leigh is allergic to cats but admits that Old Tom is very close to his heart.

MORE GREAT READING FROM PUFFIN

☆☆

I Hate Fridays! Rachel Flynn/Illustrated by Craig Smith

A collection of stories about characters in the classroom, about all the funny, sad and traumatic things that can happen. Hilariously illustrated by the very popular Craig Smith.

A Children's Book Council of Australia Notable Book, 1991.

It's Not Fair! Rachel Flynn/Illustrated by Craig Smith

More hilarious stories from the kids at Koala Hills Primary School. In this second book, following *I Hate Fridays*, you can discover more funny things about Kirsty, Sam and the others.

I Can't Wait! Rachel Flynn/Illustrated by Craig Smith

It's the last year of primary school for the characters from Koala Hills. Thadeus can finally sit with Kirsty, but is it really what he wants after all? Kerrie's dream to ride a horse comes true, but is it what she imagined? Peter gets a girlfriend, but will he ever think of anything to say to her? Following the huge success of *I Hate Fridays!* and *It's Not Fair!*, here are your favourite characters back again in grade six.

MORE GREAT READING FROM PUFFIN

☆☆☆☆☆☆☆☆☆☆☆☆☆☆☆☆☆☆☆☆☆☆☆☆☆☆☆☆☆☆☆☆☆☆

The Twenty-Seventh Annual African Hippopotamus Race
Morris Lurie/Illustrated by Elizabeth Honey

Eight-year-old Edward trains very hard for this greatest of swimming marathons with no idea of the cunning and jealousy he'll meet from the other competitors. This best-selling story takes you behind the scenes and shows you just what it takes to become a champion.

Winner of the Young Australians' Best Book Award (YABBA) 1986.

Toby's Millions Morris Lurie/Illustrated by Arthur Horner

When Toby discovers a pirate's treasure in the backyard, he finds that he, his bookworm father and scatterbrained mother must face trials and temptations they would never have imagined.

The Lenski Kids and Dracula Libby Hathorn/Illustrated by Peter Viska

The Lenski kids are the wildest, naughtiest kids in the neighbourhood – until Kim Kip arrives next door. She goes to acting school and is saving for a Harley Davidson motor bike, and is keen to do some babysitting . . .